W9-ATP-438

I dedicate this book to Michelle, Cheryl and Nico, and as always to all my grandchildren.

*Vanita Oelschlager*

ACKNOWLEDGMENTS

Mike Blanc

Kristin Blackwood

Kurt Landefeld

Paul Royer

Sheila Tarr

Jennie Levy Smith

Elaine Mesek

Michelle

Cheryl

Nico

Kelly Fogel

Carolyn Brodie

Michael Olin-Hitt

Steve Cosby

**A Tale of Two Mommies**
VanitaBooks, LLC

Text by Vanita Oelschlager
Illustrations by Mike Blanc
Design by Mike Blanc and Jennie Levy Smith, Trio Design & Marketing Communications
Printed in the USA
Hardcover Edition ISBN 978-0-9826366-6-4    Paperback Edition ISBN 978-0-9826366-7-1
**www.VanitaBooks.com**

# A Tale of Two Mommies

by **Vanita Oelschlager**
*illustrations* **Mike Blanc**

VanitaBooks, LLC

If you have a momma and a mommy, who fixes things when they break?

Oh, *Mommy* has all the tools. There's nothing she can't fix or make.

Who's your mom for riding a bike?

And who's your mom for flying a kite?

*Momma's* the one for riding a bike.

She's also the one for flying a kite.

Which mom is there when you want to go fishing?

Which mom helps out when Kitty goes missing?

*Mommy* helps when I want to go fishing.

*Both* mommies help when Kitty goes missing.

Glub, Glub, Glub? (Translation:)

Who's your mom when you set up your campsite?

Who's your mom for scary faces with flashlights?

*Mommy* helps to set up the campsite.

*Momma* makes great scary faces with a flashlight.

Which mom coaches your T-ball team?

Which mom's there when you've had a bad dream?

*Mommy* is the coach of my T-ball team.

*Both* mommies are there when I've had a bad dream.

Who's your mom when you're climbing a tree?

Who's your mom when you scrape your knee?

*Momma* helps me climb a tree.

*Both* moms help when I skin my knee.

Who empties your pockets at the end of the day?

Who teaches you what's the polite thing to say?

I empty my own pockets at the end of the day.

*Both* moms know what's the polite thing to say.

Does either mom like to pet a snake?

Which mom likes to bake some cake?

*Neither* mom really likes a snake.

But *Mommy* likes to bake the cakes.

Who's your mom for making beans and rice?

Who helps you out when your friends aren't nice?

*Mommy* makes me beans and rice.

And she also helps when my friends aren't nice.

Which mom sorts your collection of rocks?

Which mom is there when you just need to talk?

*I'm* the one who sorts my rocks.

Of course, *both* moms are there when I need to talk.

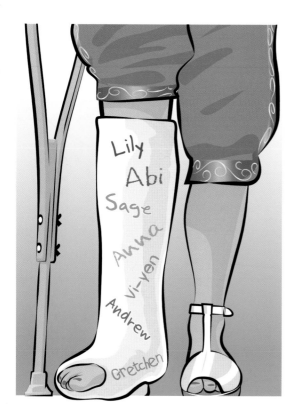

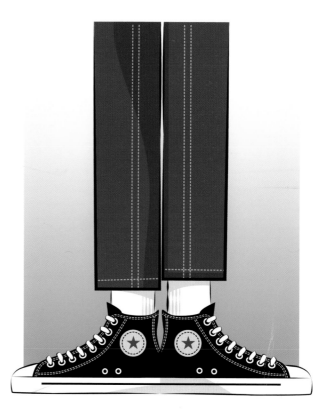

*Vanita Oelschlager* is a wife, mother, grandmother, philanthropist, former teacher, current caregiver, author and poet. A graduate of Mount Union College in Alliance, Ohio, she now serves as a Trustee of her alma mater and as Writer in Residence for the Literacy Program at The University of Akron. Vanita and her husband Jim were honored with a *Lifetime Achievement Award* from the National Multiple Sclerosis Society in 2006. She was the Congressional *Angels in Adoption* award recipient for the State of Ohio in 2007 and was named *National Volunteer of the Year* by the MS Society in 2008. Vanita was also honored in 2009 as the *Woman Philanthropist of the Year* by the Summit County Chapter of the United Way.

*Mike Blanc* is a life-long professional artist who has illustrated countless publications for both corporate and public interests worldwide. Accomplished in traditional drawing and painting techniques, he currently works almost exclusively in digital media. His first book, *Francesca*, was written by Vanita Oelschlager and published in 2008. Their second collaboration, *Postcards from a War*, followed in 2009. Additional titles with Vanita are *Bonyo Bonyo, The True Story of a Brave Boy from Kenya*, and *A Tale of Two Daddies*, both co-illustrated with associate artist Kristin Blackwood.

# About the Art

The artwork for *A Tale of Two Mommies* was developed and produced in four steps.

First: The characters were established through pencil sketches that were refined in editing sessions as the story developed. Drawings for each page were scanned into computers to form templates.

*Step 1*

Second: The artist used Adobe® Illustrator® vector-editing software to plot each shape needed to build the illustration using curve and corner points that were then adjusted, converting each sketch to a computerized version.

*Step 2*

Third: Every shape was then assigned a color attribute based on the book's color palette.

Fourth: The template was discarded and the image was fine-tuned with softening effects and transparency. Once complete, the illustrations were gathered and placed into the book design for the finished work: *A Tale of Two Mommies*.

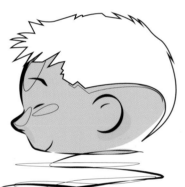

*Step 3*

# Profits

All net profits from this book will be donated to charitable organizations, with a gentle preference toward those serving people with my husband's disease – multiple sclerosis.

**Vanita Oelschlager**

*Step 4*

VanitaBooks, LLC

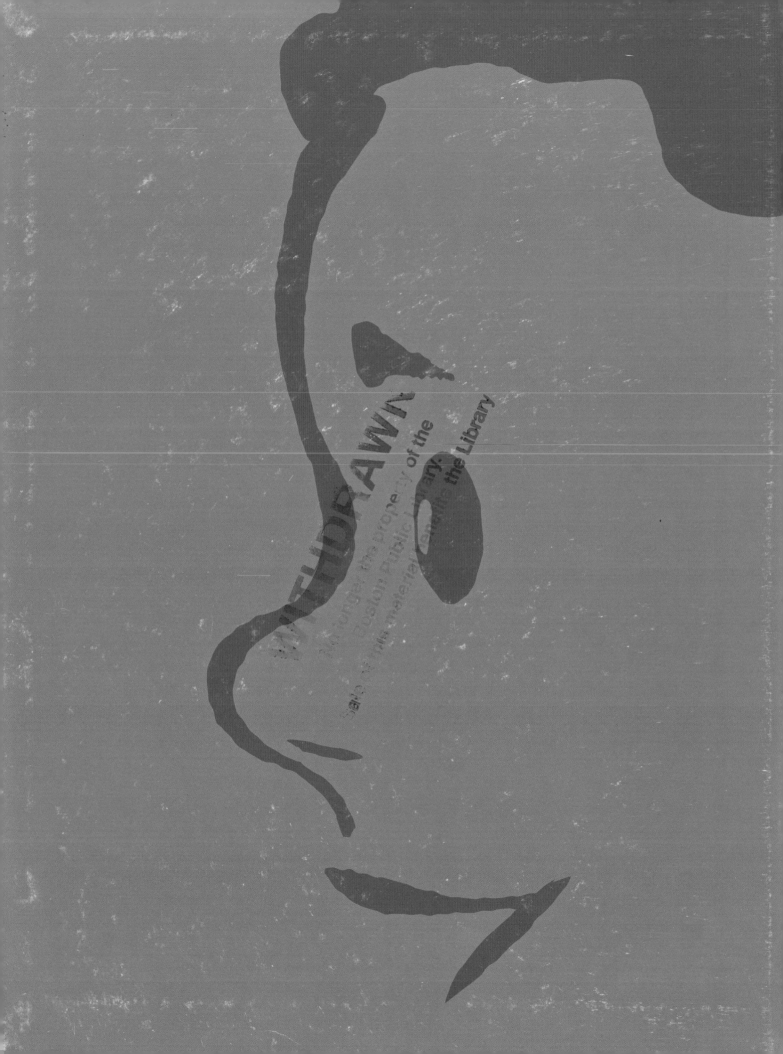